To my mother and her honey cookies – M.H.
For Richard and Rachel, with much love – A.B.

Honey Biscuits © Frances Lincoln Limited 2004
Text copyright © Meredith Hooper 1997
Illustrations copyright © Alison Bartlett 1997

This edition published in 2005 by Frances Lincoln Children's Books,
4 Torriano Mews, Torriano Ave, London NW5 2RZ

www.franceslincoln.com

Distributed in the USA by Publishers Group West

First published in the United Kingdom by Kingfisher, an imprint of Larousse plc in 1997

British Library Cataloguing in Publication Data available on request

1-84507-394-0 (HB)
1-84507-395-9 (PB)

Printed in Singapore
1 3 5 7 9 8 6 4 2

honey cookies

Meredith Hooper
Illustrated by Alison Bartlett

FRANCES LINCOLN CHILDREN'S BOOKS

Ben was cooking with his grandma.
"What should we make?" asked Ben.
"Honey cookies," said Grandma.

"What do we need?" asked Ben.
"We need…" said Grandma,

"A cow in a field eating fresh green grass,

munch,

dribble,

munch, all day long."

"A cow?" said Ben.
"And grass? For honey cookies?"
"Oh, yes!" said Grandma.
"The cow turns the grass into creamy milk."

"The milk is shaken up
and down until it turns
into smooth yellow butter."

"And half a cup of smooth
yellow butter is exactly what
we need."

"And now we need…

"Sugarcane
growing thick and tall in the warm moist earth,

until it's way, way above your head,

and as
thick
as your
wrist."

"Then it's crushed and cleaned
and boiled until it turns into
shiny little grains of white sugar."

"And two-thirds of a cup of shiny
white sugar," said Grandma,
"is exactly what we need."

"Mix the butter and
sugar together in a bowl
until they are smooth,"
said Grandma.
"The butter should not
be too hard.
It should be
nice and soft."

"What do
we need now?"
asked Ben.

"A thousand buzzing bees,"
said Grandma,
"working all day,

sucking sweet nectar

from flowers,

then flying back

to their hives

and packing
the nectar
into little
waxy cells,
where it turns
into runny
honey."

"And two tablespoons
of runny honey," said Grandma,
"is exactly what
we need."

"And now we need…

"A clucky hen, scratching around all day,

pecking up seeds and worms and tiny bugs.

She eats two handfuls of wheat, some scraps from the kitchen, and a spoonful of special food."

"Then, every morning, she lays an egg."

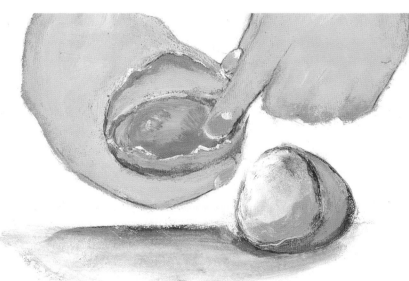

"But we don't need all of the egg," said Grandma. "We just need the yellow part, the yolk."

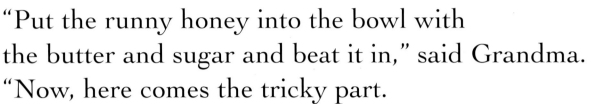

"Put the runny honey into the bowl with
the butter and sugar and beat it in," said Grandma.
"Now, here comes the tricky part.
　　　　Separating the egg yolk
　　　　　from the clear part,
　　　　　　the white, is not easy."

"You just have to learn
by doing it."

"Put the egg yolk into
the mixture," said Grandma,
"and beat it in."

"Now what do we need?"
asked Ben.

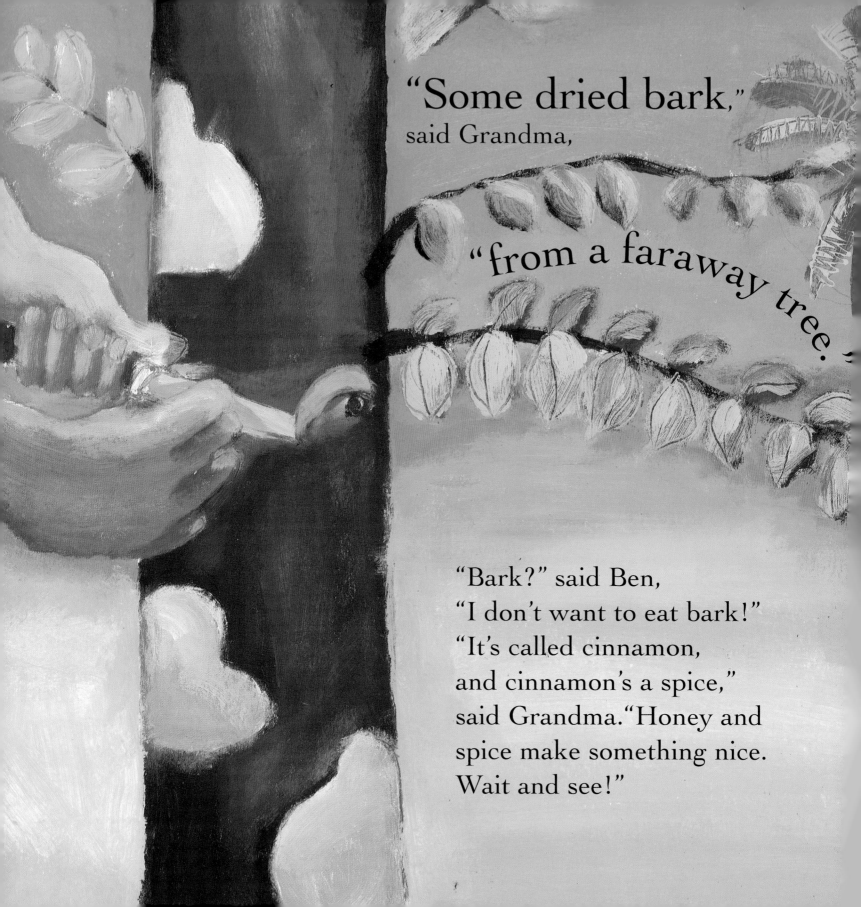

"Some dried bark,"
said Grandma,

"from a faraway tree."

"Bark?" said Ben,
"I don't want to eat bark!"
"It's called cinnamon,
and cinnamon's a spice,"
said Grandma. "Honey and
spice make something nice.
Wait and see!"

"The bark is ground up into brown powder."

"And that's exactly what we need," said Grandma, "a level teaspoonful of brown powdery cinnamon."

"And now we need…

"A field of golden wheat,

with stalks full of seeds ripening in the sun."

"The seeds are ground up
to make soft white flour."

"And one and three-quarters
cups of soft white flour,"
said Grandma, "is exactly
what we need."

"Put the cinnamon into the mixture,"
said Grandma. "Then add the flour little by little,
but don't beat it too much."

"Now we've made a soft dough.
Here comes the good part. Ready?"

"Take a small piece of dough, roll it quickly in your hands,

and make a little ball."

"Roll the ball in some shiny white sugar and cinnamon."

"Then put it on the cookie sheet."

"You have to give each little
ball a bit of space," said Grandma.
"Why?" asked Ben.
"Wait and see," said Grandma.

"Remember, the oven shouldn't be too hot or too cool. It has to be just right to cook honey cookies." Grandma pulled on the oven mitts and put the sheet of little balls in the oven.

Soon, a wonderful spicy smell filled the kitchen.

"Let's take a peek," said Grandma. "We need to see how our honey cookies are doing." The balls of dough had disappeared. They had turned into round, flat, golden-brown cookies. Grandma put on her oven mitts and took the hot cookie sheet out of the oven.

"Let the honey cookies cool, just for a minute or two," said Grandma.

"My honey cookies,"
said Ben,
"have needed
a cow,
a thousand bees,
and a hen…

a field of sugarcane,
a field of wheat,
and part of a tree."

"And we've needed
the help of
fresh green grass and
bright-colored flowers,"
said Grandma.

"And we've needed
the good earth,
the warm sun,
and the rain."

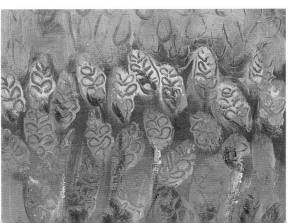

But Ben could not
say anything.
His mouth
was too full of

warm, yummy

honey
cookie.

Honey Cookies

To make honey cookies, you need:
1/2 cup butter
2/3 cup sugar
2 tablespoons honey
1 egg yolk
1 level teaspoon cinnamon
1 3/4 cups self-rising flour

- Beat the butter and sugar together in a bowl until they are creamy. (You can use an electric mixer.)
- Next, beat in the honey, then the egg yolk.
- Add the cinnamon and flour and mix into a soft dough. If the dough is sticky, add a little more flour.
- Shape about a teaspoon of dough into a ball, roll it in a little extra sugar and cinnamon, and put it on a greased cookie sheet. The mixture should make about 30 cookies.
- Put the biscuits into an oven heated to 350 F for 12 to 15 minutes.

The cookies are ready when they are golden-brown. Take the cookies out of the oven, let them settle for a few minutes, then put them on to a rack or a plate to cool.